To Jennifer
for always believing in me
~ Julia

CLIQUES Just Don't Make Cents

Written by
Julia Cook

Illustrated by
Anita DuFalla

Boys Town, Nebraska

Cliques Just Don't Make Cents!

ISBN 978-1-934490-39-6

Published by the Boys Town Press
14100 Crawford St.
Boys Town, NE 68010

For a Boys Town Press catalog, call **1-800-282-6657**
or visit our website: **BoysTownPress.org**

Publisher's Cataloging-in-Publication Data

Cook, Julia, 1964-

Cliques just don't make cents! / written by Julia Cook ; illustrated by Anita DuFalla. -- Boys Town, NE : Boys Town Press, c2012.

p. ; cm.
(Building relationships ; 2nd)

ISBN: 978-1-934490-39-6

Audience: grades 3-8.
Summary: Penny tries to hang with the Coin Clique, but she usually feels left out. Then one day Penny lands in a pocket with the beautiful, gold Dollar coin, who starts to teach Penny how special and valuable she really is. Included in the book are tips for parents, teachers, and counselors on how to help young people, especially girls, who feel excluded and left out by others.

1. Cliques (Sociology)--Juvenile fiction. 2. Popularity--Juvenile fiction. 3. Self-esteem in children--Juvenile fiction. 4. Interpersonal relations in children--Juvenile fiction. 5. Children--Life skills guides--Juvenile fiction. 6. [Cliques (Sociology)--Fiction. 7. Popularity--Fiction. 8. Self-esteem--Fiction. 9. Interpersonal relations--Fiction.] I. DuFalla, Anita. II. Title. III. Series: Building relationships ; no. 2..

PZ7.C76984 C55 2012

E 1208

Printed in the United States
10 9 8 7 6 5 4 3 2 1

Boys Town Press is the publishing division of Boys Town, a national organization serving children and families.

My name is **Penny.**

I'm one of the coins.

Being a coin can be fun. We get flipped and tossed and jingled.

We get to travel a lot... mostly in pockets.

Some people like to save us. They sometimes keep us in banks that look like pigs. People are weird!

But most people don't hang onto us very long. They spend us fast!

It's almost like we're burning holes in their pockets.

I hang out with the other coins.
They are my friends ... well, kind of.

There's **Half Dollar** – she's bigger than me, and shinier than me.

All of the coins look up to her. She likes to tell everyone what to do and how to roll. She has cool ridges.

When we get stacked, **Half Dollar** is always on the bottom. She says it's because she's worth the most.

Then, there's **Quarter**. She has ridges too.
She and **Half Dollar** are best friends. They do everything together.

Quarter tries to be just like **Half Dollar**.
She tries to roll like her.
She tries to shine like her.
She even says everything that **Half Dollar** says and she always tries to say it the exact same way.

Next, there's **Dime**.
She's tiny, cute and perfect.
She hardly weighs anything.
She shines really bright and she has tiny little ridges.

Everyone likes **Dime**.
She even has friends that aren't coins.
She talks to the money clip and even hangs
out with the cell phone sometimes.

Dime is so little that once in a while,
she accidentally gets tossed out of our pocket
and lands on the floor … but she always gets picked up.

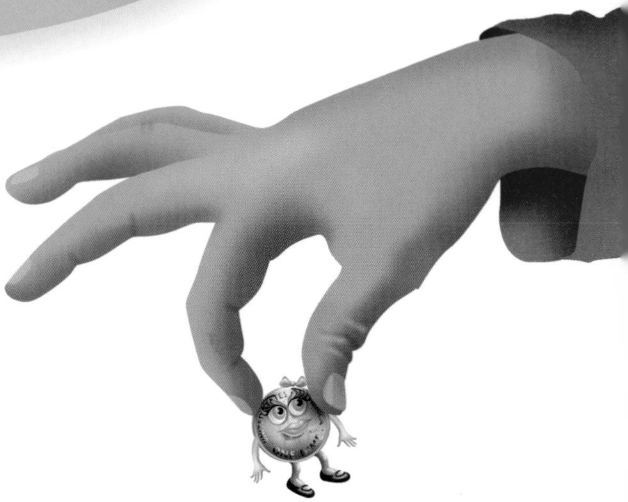

My other friend is **Nickel**. She's kind of like the rest of the coins because she's silver, but she's a little bit like me too because she doesn't have ridges.

Nickel and I are the only two coins with the smooth edges. We both wish we had ridges, but we don't.

Nickel is my best friend, but sometimes she hangs out more with **Dime** and **Quarter** than she does with me.

I try to hang out with the silvers.
I do everything that **Half Dollar** tells me to do,
and I try to roll like the others.
But since I don't have ridges and I'm not silver,
I just can't seem to roll like they do.

Nickel can't roll like the rest of the coins either,
but since she's silver, it's easier for her.

Half Dollar and **Quarter** told me that I'm not worth much.
They say that if they had their way, they'd just get rid of me.

But people still keep clumping us all together,
so I'm sort of forced to hang out with them.

It's not like I feel that I can go out and find other friends like **Dime** does,
so I just do the best that I can and I try to fit in.

Last week, **Quarter** and **Half Dollar** got into a big fight.

Quarter started to brag that she got to be used in the pop machine.

She told **Half Dollar** that she was more popular because she is the most common coin used by people.

Half Dollar felt really bad, so I gave her a big hug and told her that I thought she was AMAZING! She let me hang out with her for a little while.

Then, she wrote a note to **Quarter** and told me to take it to her, so I did. She even told me that I could read it if I wanted to.

Dear Quarter,
There might be more of you out there,
But keep this fact in mind,
I'm worth twice as much as you,
so you'd better start being kind.

If you didn't have me to follow around
You wouldn't be nearly as cool.
You better start rolling the right way with me
or I'll make you look like a fool!

Half Dollar

Quarter, who has NEVER been nice,
actually talked to me and tried to get me to see her side.

"Don't you think I'm more popular than **Half Dollar**?
Dime and **Nickel** say I am."

"I think that you are AMAZING!" I said.

I was in heaven! Both **Quarter** and **Half Dollar** were actually talking to ME!

A few minutes later,
a hand came into the pocket
and scooped **Quarter**
and **Half Dollar** out,
leaving the rest of us behind.

I don't exactly know what happened,
but the next day when they came back,
they were very best friends again,
and neither of them would give me the time of day.

A few days ago, a hand was reaching for the cell phone,
and when it came out of the pocket, so did I.
I landed heads up on the floor.

This happens to **Dime** all of the time, I thought.
And she always gets picked up.

But nobody picked me up, so I just sat there
all by myself for two very long days.

Maybe **Quarter** was right, I thought.
I don't have ridges and I'm not even silver...
Why would anyone waste their time bending down to pick me up?

Just when I was about to give up all hope,
I heard a voice say, "Heads-Up **Penny**!
That's good luck!"

Before I knew it, a hand picked me up
and put me into a different pocket.

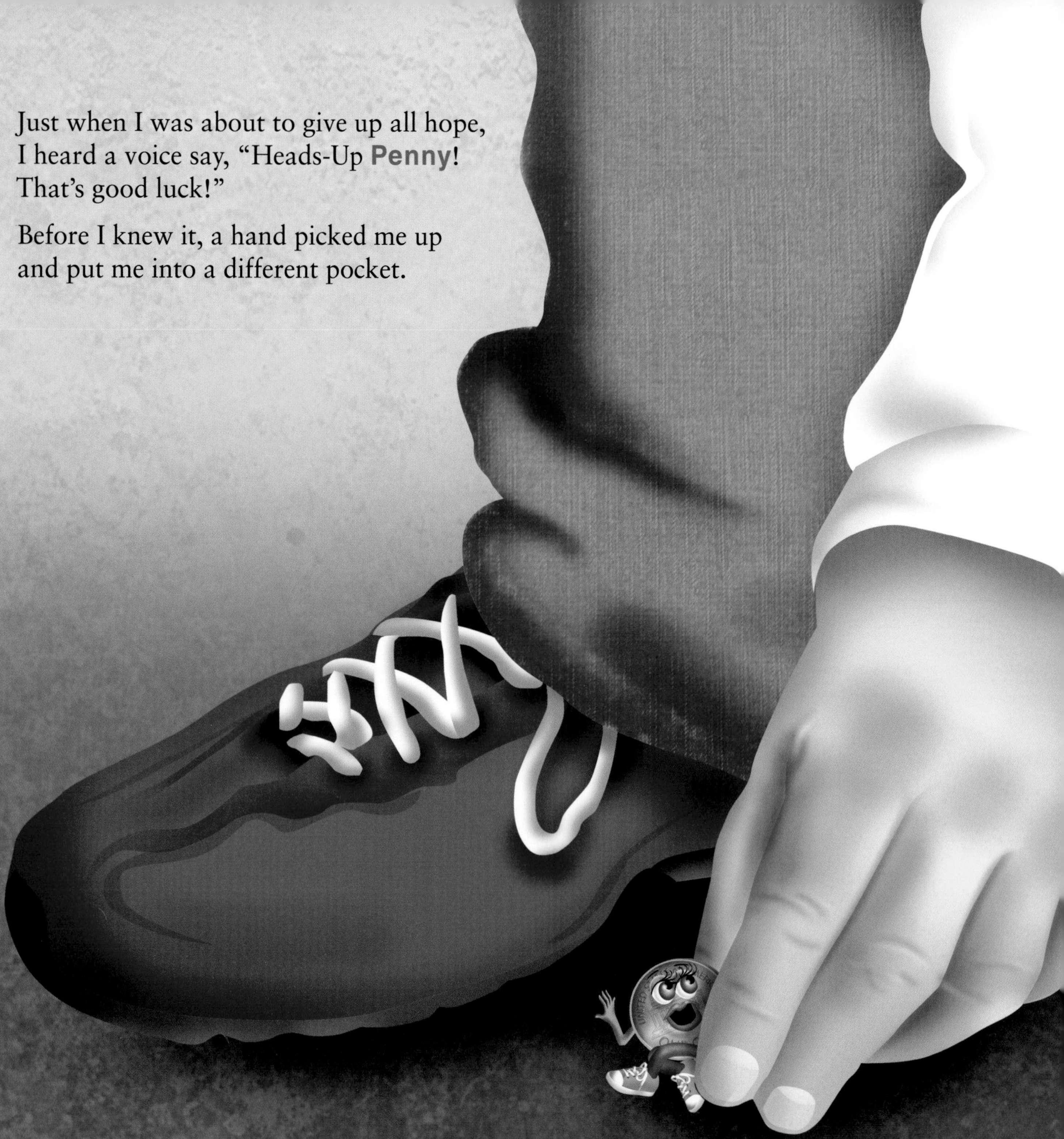

I looked up and
saw the most beautiful coin
I had ever laid eyes on.

"Hi **Penny!**" she said. "How are you?"

"Who are you?" I asked.

"I'm **Dollar**. I'm a gold dollar coin."

"WOW! I've never seen a coin like you!
You're BEAUTIFUL!"

"Thanks! You're not so bad yourself."

"Yeah right," I said. "I'm not worth much, I'm not silver, and I don't have ridges. It's not like I can exactly roll with the other coins."

“So… the Coin Clique has made you feel bad, huh?

Let me tell you something **Penny**.
I don’t have ridges, I’m not silver, and I’m actually worth more than all of the other coins put together – you included!
But that doesn’t mean that I’m too good to roll with you.

YOU are a penny!
You’re very special and I am proud to call you my friend.”

"Well, I don't feel very special," I said.

"Listen to me, **Penny**.
You are the only coin that has any cents (except for me that is).
You are also the only coin who is lucky when you land heads up.

Your copper color makes you unique, and it's beautiful on you!"

"You get to have Abraham Lincoln's face plastered to your side.
That means you are a symbol for honesty.

Did you know that when Abraham Lincoln was a young store clerk,
he walked three miles to give six pennies just like you
to a customer that he had overcharged?

What an honor!"

"**Penny**, you also symbolize saving money for people.

Haven't you ever heard the phrases
'A penny saved is a penny earned,' and
'Pinching pennies can make a difference'?

People would never say,
'A quarter saved is a quarter earned,'
... and nobody's ever pinched a half dollar!"

"Gee! I never thought about it like that," I said.

"Without you, **Penny**, paying exact change
for an item costing $5.98 would be impossible!
The store clerk would have to round the price up and charge $6.00.
Then people would end up paying more for everything!

If we didn't have you, we'd have even more inflation!"

"You even help people talk
about their feelings
... like when a person says
'A penny for your thoughts.'

I've never heard anyone
say, 'A dime or a nickel
for your thoughts.'"

"Most important of all, **Penny**, you need to realize that your value in life has nothing to do with how much you can buy!"

All of a sudden, my insides went from worthless to worthy!

Dollar grabbed a handkerchief that was in the pocket with us, and taught me how to give myself a shine.

"If you're going to roll with me, you have to believe in yourself, and you have to be proud to be different!"

When I got done polishing up, I hardly recognized myself! Then, the coolest thing happened ... not only did I shine on the outside, I felt shiny on the inside too!

The next day, all the coins ended up in the same pocket.

The silvers couldn't take their eyes off of **Dollar,** and they couldn't believe that she was my friend!

Nickel and **Dime** noticed my new shine and told me I looked great!

I even got up enough guts to introduce myself to the cell phone and the money clip. They were really nice! They even invited me to hang out with them sometime!

From that day on,
I was no longer just a penny.
I was no longer just a coin.

I was
CHANGE!

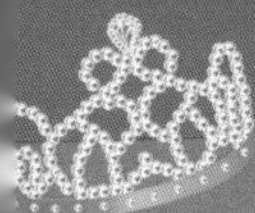

Tips for Parents and Educators

Cliques are everywhere – from the childhood playground to the adult workplace. They are a part of human nature in every society and have existed since the beginning of mankind. Unlike a friendship group, where members often welcome other people to join in, a clique will have a strict code of membership and member expectations. People belonging to a clique will often only associate with other clique members. In comparison, a regular "group of friends" is open to members socializing with those outside of the group.

People join cliques for a number of reasons including: social status and acceptance, fear of being left out, opportunities to be in control of others, and having the security of being in a place where the rules on "how to act" are clearly defined.

Cliques are very hard for EVERYONE (those on the inside and those on the outside), and they are not going away…so here are a few tips on how to deal with them:

- Teach children to maintain their sense of self-worth and get in touch with their own values, interests, and opinions.
- Help kids understand that a clique is not all that it seems. Many times the leader and members of a clique are insecure and unhappy. Members may also choose to belong because they are too scared to leave.
- Encourage kids to participate in activities that make them feel good about themselves.
- Help the Pennies, Dimes, and Nickels of the world to look outside the clique to find other friends.
- Encourage all children to develop a strong sense of self and to form their own opinions of others.
- Create a safe environment (at home and in school) where kids are encouraged to include everyone and cliques are not validated.

For more parenting information, visit:

parenting.org℠ *from* BOYS TOWN.

Other Boys Town Press Books by Julia Cook

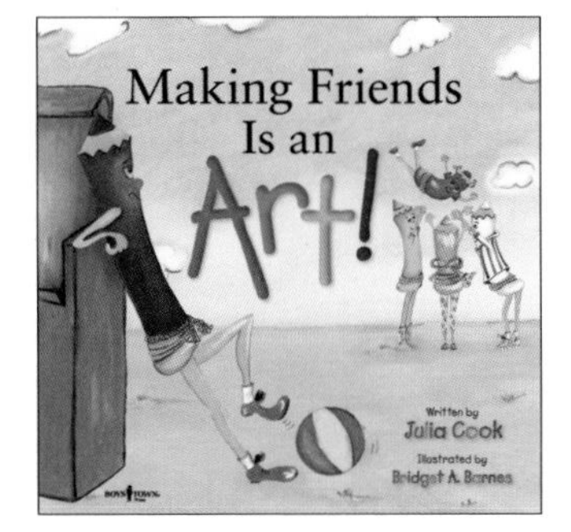

ISBN 978-1-934490-30-3

ISBN 978-1-934490-34-1

ISBN 978-1-934490-20-4

ISBN 978-1-934490-25-9

ISBN 978-1-934490-28-0

TEAMWORK Isn't My Thing, and I Don't Like to SHARE!

ISBN 978-1-934490-35-8

ISBN 978-1-934490-23-5

ISBN 978-1-934490-27-3

ISBN 978-1-934490-32-7

ISBN 978-1-934490-37-2

Boys Town Education and Parenting Programs

For more information on Boys Town, its Education Model, Common Sense Parenting® and training programs, visit BoysTown.org/educators, BoysTown.org/parents, or parenting.org, e-mail training@BoysTown.org, or call 1-800-545-5771.

For parenting and educational books and other resources, visit the Boys Town Press website at BoysTownPress.org, e-mail btpress@BoysTown.org, or call 1-800-282-6657.

BoysTownPress.org